A Diplodocus Trampled My Teepee

SAURUS STREET

A Diplodocus Trampled My Teepee

Nick Falk and
Tony Flowers

RANDOM HOUSE AUSTRALIA

To Chris K, for bringing Saurus Street to life
— Nick Falk

For friends and family, who are always there in the
good times and the bad — Tony Flowers

A Random House book
Published by Random House Australia Pty Ltd
Level 3, 100 Pacific Highway, North Sydney NSW 2060
www.randomhouse.com.au

First published by Random House Australia in 2013

Addresses for companies within the Random House Group can be found at
www.randomhouse.com.au/offices

National Library of Australia
Cataloguing-in-Publication Entry

Author: Falk, Nicholas
Title: A diplodocus trampled my teepee / Nick Falk; Tony Flowers, Illustrator
ISBN: 978 0 85798 184 4 (pbk)
Series: Falk, Nicholas. Saurus street; 6
Target Audience: For primary school age
Subjects: Diplodocus – Juvenile fiction
Other Authors/Contributors: Flowers, Tony
Dewey Number: A823.4

Cover and internal illustrations by Tony Flowers
Internal design and typesetting by Anna Warren, Warren Ventures
Printed in Australia by Griffin Press, an accredited ISO AS/NZS 14001:2004 Environmental
Management System printer

Random House Australia uses papers that are natural, renewable and recyclable products and made
from wood grown in sustainable forests. The logging and manufacturing processes are expected to
conform to the environmental regulations of the country of origin.

CHAPTER ONE
Imagineering

'Wake up, Toby. It's time to inspect our treasure.'

I open my eyes and sit up. Jack's already awake. His dad and his **scary** sister, Saffi, are asleep in their sleeping bags. The coast is clear.

Jack unzips his stegosaurus schoolbag. That's where we put all the

treasures we found on the beach today. He empties it onto the floor of the teepee. That's what we're camping in. A great **big** family-sized teepee. Jack's dad made it out of branches, ropes and plastic sheets.

This is the first time I've ever been camping. We're at Camp Saurus, which is in the woods near Saurus Sands. Saffi thinks it's silly camping so close to home. But I don't. I think it's exciting. Especially like now, at night, when it's dark outside.

I can look up at the sky and see about a million stars. And each star is a sun in a solar system billions of miles away. It's amazing.

My parents don't like camping.

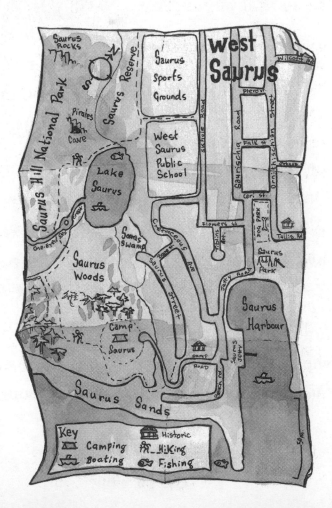

That's why
I've never
been before,
but Jack's
family loves
it.

Jack's my best friend. He lives just up the road from me on Saurus Street, and we've known each other since we were babies. We love going on **adventures** together. Once we even travelled back in time. When Jack's around, everything's an adventure.

'Wow,' says Jack. 'Look at this.' He's holding up a long, **pointy**, twisty shell. 'It's a mongosaurus tooth,' he adds. 'Mongosauruses were water dinosaurs.

They had laser eyes and their scales could turn **invisible**.'

We're playing 'Imagineering'. Imagineering is when you find treasure and then you make up a special story about it. To win at Imagineering you've got to make the other person believe that your story's true. Jack's really good at Imagineering.

He's got an awesome *imagination*.

I'm not so good. I'm better at facts than imaginary stuff. But I still like playing.

I pick up a piece of green glass worn

smooth

by the sea.

'This,' I say, 'is a Moggle-Boggle. It's a magic mirror used by mermaids to see if their tails are stuck on properly.'

Jack laughs.

'Good one,' he says.

I like it when I make Jack laugh.

That's what being friends is all about.

Suddenly Jack gasps. 'Look at this!' He picks up an old hook.

'What is it?' I ask.

Jack looks at me. His eyes are deadly serious. 'It's a deinonychus claw,'

he says. 'A real fossilised deinonychus claw.'

I've heard of the deinonychus. Its name means 'Terrible Claw' in Latin. (Latin is a really old language that no-one uses anymore. The Romans used to speak in Latin.) And that's what the deinonychus had: a **TERRIBLE** claw on each foot, to rip open its prey. Deinonychus was one of the deadliest dinosaurs that ever lived.

But that hook isn't *really* a deinonychus claw. Jack's just trying to win at Imagineering. Acting like it's real is all part of the game.

I grin. 'Nice try,' I say.

Jack grins too. He thought he had me.

My turn again. I pick up an old metal lid. I try to look serious. 'It's a fish frisbee,' I explain. 'School fish use it to play catch at lunchtimes.'

Jack giggles. 'Fish can't catch. They haven't got hands!'

His turn. He picks up a tiny wooden box. It's old, black and **roffen**. It looks like it's been sitting at the bottom of the sea for a very long time.

Jack opens the box. He gasps. 'I can't believe it,' he says.

He's acting again. I wonder what he's going to come up with this time?

Jack turns the box around. There's something round and

inside. It looks a bit like a marble.

'This,' whispers Jack, 'is the lost eyeball of Captain Saurus.'

CHAPTER TWO

The Legend of Captain Saurus

I wait for Jack to smile. But he doesn't.

He doesn't even . I told you he was good at this game.

'I'm serious,' he says. 'It really *is* . . .'

'Is what?' I ask.

'Is what I said it is,' says Jack.

'What?' I grin. 'You mean the lost eyeball of Captain Saur–'

'*SHHHH*,' hisses Jack. 'Don't say it again. Don't you remember the curse?'

Of course I do. All the kids on Saurus Street know about the **curse**.

Captain Saurus was the most

famous pirate who ever lived. He was the dinosaur pirate. His ship was made of diplodocus bones, he had a stegosaurus spike leg stump and a curved allosaurus tooth instead of a hand.

And Captain Saurus had a glass eye. A **magic** glass eye. Legend has it he could see his enemies with that eye, even in the dead of night. And when he

was finally defeated by the dreaded Pirate Bloodbreath, the glass eye fell into the sea and Captain Saurus

put a **curse** on it. *'He who finds my eye and says my name three times will bring my bones back to life . . .'*

But I know Jack's joking. He's just trying to win at Imagineering. And I'm not that gullible.

'You're being **silly**,' I say.

'That is so *not* the lost eyeball of Captain Saurus.'

'Stop it,' says Jack. 'That's twice now! If we say his name three times, the curse comes true!'

I roll my eyes. He's taking it a bit far.

I reach over and pick up the marble. It's round and yellow and . And it's got a black dot in the middle. It looks a bit like the pupil of a . . . *WHOA! This really IS an eyeball.*

I stare at Jack. 'Are you serious?' I whisper.

'Yes,' says Jack. 'I'm serious.'

'We're not playing Imagineering anymore?'

'No,' hisses Jack. 'We're not.'

Wow. This is amazing. I look at

the eyeball again. I wonder what it's made of? I shine my torch on it. Just as I thought. The eyeball splits the light into all the colours of the rainbow. That's called refraction. And that means this eyeball is made of crystal. (I learnt about refraction at science camp last year. Light is made of lots of different colours. And when they mix together they turn into normal see-through light. It's really clever.)

'Check it out,' **whispers** Jack.

I look to where Jack's pointing. There's tiny writing engraved on the back of the eyeball. 'ENIM SI TAHW KCAB EVIG,

ESRUC EHT ESREVER OT,' it reads.

'What does it mean?' asks Jack.

'I'm not sure,' I say, 'but I think it's written in Latin. "ENIM" means "For" and "SI" means "if".'

'What does the rest of it say then?' asks Jack.

I read the eyeball again. 'I don't know. I don't recognise any of the words. Maybe it's spelt wrong? Pirates aren't very good at spelling.'

'I can't believe you two woke me up talking about pirates!'

I spin around.

Saffi, Jack's 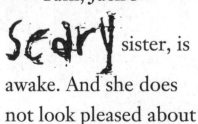 sister, is awake. And she does not look pleased about

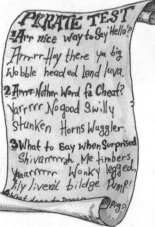

PIRATE TEST

1 Arr nice way to Say Hello?
Armrr Hoy there ya big
Wobble headed land luva.

2 Arr Nother Word fa Cheat?
Yarrrrr No good Swilly
Stunken Horns Waggler.

3 What to Say when Surprised
Shivarrrrah Me timbers,
Yaarrrrr Wonky legged
ily livered bildge Pump!

16

being woken up in the middle of the night.

'What are you two idiots fiddling with?' Saffi snaps. She reaches out and snatches the eyeball. Her lip curls. 'Yuck,' she says. 'That's completely **dis gus tin g**.'

'Give it back!' says Jack.

'Why should I?' she sneers.

'Because it's precious!' says Jack.

Saffi snorts. 'You're such babies,' she says. 'What do you think it is? The lost eyeball of Captain Saurus or something?' She tosses it across the teepee. 'Go to sleep,' she **growls**, '*and stop talking.*' Saffi curls back into her sleeping bag.

I turn to Jack. His face has gone **white**. He picks up the eyeball, fingers shaking, and puts it back in the box.

'What's wrong?' I whisper.

After all, that could have been a lot worse. For Saffi, that was almost friendly.

'Don't you realise what just happened?' whispers Jack.

'What?' I say.

'She said his name. For the third time. Saffi just activated the **curse**!'

CHAPTER THREE
Toe Muncher

I wake up. It's finally morning. I feel exhausted.

We were up most of the night waiting for Captain Saurus to come and get us. I don't really believe in curses, but then Jack started talking about skeletons and swords and **ghostly** ghouls. And after that, neither of us could sleep.

'Come on,' says Jack. 'Let's go investigate.'

I like the sound of that. Investigating is one of my favourite things.

We crawl out of our sleeping bags and get dressed as quietly as we can.

We don't want to wake up Saffi. Mornings are her scariest time. Legend has it that Saffi smiled once. But that's one legend no-one believes.

We tiptoe out of the teepee. It's raining. Not very hard, but hard enough to make a rainbow. Rainbows are made when sunlight shines through raindrops. Refraction again. Refraction is cool.

'Where's your dad?' I ask.

'Swimming,' says Jack. 'He always does that in the mornings.'

'Even when it's raining?' I ask.

'Even when it's **SNOWING**,' says Jack.

We zip up our jackets and start investigating the camp site.

'What are we looking for?' I ask. A good investigator always knows what he's searching for.

'Footprints,' says Jack. 'If Captain Saurus came in the night, he'd have left footprints. Everything with feet makes footprints. Even skeletons.'

I keep investigating but I don't expect to find anything. Jack's got a wilder *imagination* than me. He believes in curses and legends and fairytales. But I don't. I'm a science nut, so I know the truth about legends. They're just stories. And stories don't come true.

'Quickly!' Jack calls out. 'Over here!'

I rush towards him. Could I be

wrong? Has he really found a skeleton footprint?

No. Instead, he's found a puddle. A big, **MUDDY** one.

What's so amazing about that? I step closer. Suddenly something lunges out of the puddle and tries to grab my toes.

'Yikes!' I jump backwards.

There's a weird-looking squid thing in the water. It's got a big *spiral* shell with tentacles sticking out the front.

'What is it?' I ask.

Jack leans down and lifts the squid thing carefully out of the puddle. Jack's good with animals. Even big ones, like dinosaurs.

24

'I can't believe it,' he says. 'It's an ammonite!'

'A what?' I say.

'An ammonite,' he repeats. 'A type of shellfish.'

I peer at the ammonite. 'Shellfish aren't supposed to be in puddles.'

'This thing's not even supposed to be *alive*,' says Jack. 'Ammonites are extinct. They're supposed to be fossils.'

The ammonite's little tentacles are **wriggling**. It doesn't look much like a fossil.

'So what's it doing here?' I ask.

Jack shakes his head. 'I don't know,' he says. 'It's completely **weird**.' He puts the ammonite gently back where he found it.

And that's when someone starts screaming.

26

CHAPTER FOUR
Attack of the Chicken-Lizard

Jack and I race back towards the teepee. That's where the screaming's coming from.

When we get there we find Saffi outside, **hopping** from foot to foot in her pyjamas.

'There's something in there!' she shrieks.

'What is it?' asks Jack.

'Some . . . *thing*,' chokes Saffi.

We stop and listen. There are definitely sounds coming from inside the teepee. Scraping, scritching, scratching sounds.

'It's him,' whispers Jack. He looks
at me with wide eyes. 'It's Captain
Saurus.'

RRR R I P. There's
a tearing sound from inside the
teepee. The sound of a skeleton pirate
slicing open a sleeping bag.
I can't believe it. The curse really did
come true.

'Stand back,'
says a voice from
behind us.
'I'm going in.'

It's Jack's dad.
He's back from the
beach. He marches
towards the teepee in his
banana-yellow swimming trunks.

But at the last moment I jump in front of him. I can't let Jack's dad get **skewered**. After all, it's one-third my fault there's an undead pirate in the teepee. I'm the one who said his name the second time.

'I'll come with you,' says Jack.

His dad's about to object, but we don't give him the chance. Jack and I take a **deep** breath and march into the teepee.

30

It's dark inside. It takes our eyes a few seconds to adjust from the bright morning sun.

'Where is he?' whispers Jack.

We look around. For a great big deadly pirate, Captain Saurus is very good at hiding.

'There!' I say.

Something's moving underneath my sleeping bag. Whatever it is looks rather small. Maybe Captain Saurus is a tiny pirate? Or perhaps just some of his bones came back to life? If he's only got legs and a head, he's going to look

ridiculous.

'Ready?' says Jack. 'On three.'

We tiptoe towards the sleeping bag. The thing underneath stops moving. Now it just looks like a lump. It's still there, though. It's probably waiting to leap out and get us.

'One,' whispers Jack.

We bend our knees.

'Two,' whispers Jack.

We grab hold of the sleeping bag.

'THREE!'

We pull the sleeping bag away.

SQUAAAWK!

Something springs towards us. Something small and green with claws and teeth and feathers.

Feathers? I don't remember anything

about Captain Saurus having feathers. Maybe we've brought his parrot back to life instead? A zombie pirate-parrot. That's something you don't see every day.

Brains

The feathered creature darts across the teepee and tucks itself behind a rucksack.

It looks a bit scared.

We **creep** over towards it. I grab hold of a cooking ladle. Just in case it bites.

Zombie pirate-parrot bites could be lethal. We peer over the rucksack.

There's a brightly coloured reptile hiding behind it. It's green and red and blue, and it's got yellow feathers running up its arms. It's standing on its back legs, peering at us. It looks a bit like a chicken crossed with a lizard.

'**GRRRR**,'

growls the chicken-lizard, baring its claws. It's got a high-pitched squeaky voice.

'I can't believe it,' says Jack. 'It's a microraptor!'

CHAPTER FIVE
A Lesser-Spotted What?

'Is everyone okay?' Jack's dad charges into the teepee. He's clutching a kayak paddle, ready to **THWAP** anything dangerous. But there's nothing dangerous to **THWAP**.

'Goodness me,' he says, dropping the paddle. 'What's that?'

36

The microraptor squawks at him. For a dinosaur, it's really not that scary. Imagine how **scared** they must have been, living at the same time as great big T-rexes!

'It's a microraptor,' says Jack.

'A micro-whatter?' says Jack's dad.

'A microraptor,' repeats Jack. 'A teeny tiny dinosaur. They lived in the early Cretaceous period.'

'Ha ha,' says Jack's dad. 'Now that *really would* be a discovery.'

He approaches the microraptor, reaching forward with a finger.

SNAP!

The dinosaur gives him a nasty nip.

'Ooh!' Jack's dad grins, shaking his hand. 'Feisty little fella, isn't he? I wonder what he is?' He rushes out of the teepee to find his lizard book.

Jack and I watch the microraptor as it starts chewing Saffi's clothes.

'What's it doing here?' asks Jack.

'I don't know,' I say. 'Did you wish upon a star again?'

Once Jack saw a shooting star and wished for a dinosaur. And it came true.

His wishes are super **POWERFUL**.

'No,' says Jack. 'I didn't even see a shooting star.'

I think for a minute. I'm good at thinking. Mostly because I wear glasses. Glasses **magnify** your thoughts.

'I've got it!' I say.

'What?' says Jack, as the micro-raptor swallows a sock.

'It's the Captain Saurus **curse**! Remember the words? *"He who finds my eye and says my name three times will bring my bones back to life"*.'

Jack looks confused. 'But his bones haven't come back to life.'

'*His* bones haven't,' I say, 'but his dinosaur bones have! The ammonite and the microraptor must have belonged to Captain Saurus!'

'Excellent!' says Jack's dad, bursting back into the teepee. 'It's still here!' He's flicking through a book called *Lizards of Australia*. 'Now,' he mutters, 'what are you? A bearded dragon? A long-necked skink? AHA! I've got it!' He grins, hugely excited. 'It's a Lesser-Spotted Gibber Lizard!' He shows us the page.

'*Lesser-Spotted Gibber Lizard. Exceedingly rare*,' it says. The picture in the book looks nothing like the microraptor.

'This is marvellous,'

says Jack's dad. 'A Lesser-Spotted Gibber Lizard. And such a big one!'

'It's not a Gibber Lizard, Dad,' says Jack. 'And it's not that big, either. I think some much bigger lizards are about to turn up.'

Jack's probably right. I bet ammonites and microraptors weren't the only bones Captain Saurus collected.

'Nonsense!' says Jack's dad.

41

'There aren't any bigger lizards around here. This little fella's the find of the century! We'll get an article in *Lizards Today* for sure!' He

hurries out of the teepee to find his camera.

Jack and I stare at the microraptor. It's finished with the socks and it's started on the soft toys.

'Give that back!' snaps Saffi.

She darts forward and snatches her teddy bear back. Saffi might be sixteen, but

she still likes teddies. She turns and scowls at Jack. 'What did you mean when you said **bigger** ones were about to turn up?'

'Exactly what I said,' says Jack. 'That one's just a tiddler.'

The microraptor stops chewing. It looks a bit offended.

'What are you talking about?' snaps Saffi. 'What kind of lizard could possibly be bigger than that?'

BOOM!

We all rush out of the teepee. Jack's dad is staring into the forest. It looks like something's pushing its way through the trees. Something very large.

'What is going on?!' moans Saffi.

BOOM!

The whole ground starts shaking. The microraptor squawks and hides behind my legs.

'Nothing to worry about,' says Jack's dad, nervously. 'It's probably just a big kangaroo.'

KABOOM!

That's no kangaroo. Jack and I take a step backwards. So does the microraptor. Jack's dad gawps up at the treetops. There's a huge head rising up into the sky. A huge head on a truly enormous neck.

It's a diplodocus.

'Goodness,' croaks Jack's dad. 'Now that really *is* a big lizard.'

44

CHAPTER SIX
Trampled Underfoot

'*MOVE!*' shouts Saffi. She pushes her dad to one side.

And just in time too. A gigantic diplodocus foot crunches to the ground, right where he was standing.

THUMP!

Another diplodocus foot smashes down to the left of us. The teepee gets

flattened. Oh well.
There goes our treasure
collection.

'We've got to get
out of here!'
shrieks Saffi.

We turn
around and start
racing down the
hill. The micro-
raptor leads the
way. Hopefully it
knows where it's
going. I certainly
don't.

SMASH!

A gigantic tail slams into a ghost
gum, sending the tree crashing to the

ground behind us.

'What did you two do?' screams Saffi.

'It was the eyeball,' gasps Jack. 'It's brought his dinosaurs back to life.'

'Whose dinosaurs?' shouts Saffi.

'Captain Saurus's!' says Jack.

A massive foot thumps into the ground right in front of us, sending us sprawling to the floor.

'How do we send them back again?' groans Saffi.

That's a good question. If a diplodocus has come back to life, then who knows what other prehistoric giants are lurking in the forest?

A deafening sound fills the air. I look down. The ground is starting to split in two. The diplodocus has cracked the earth!

'DAD!' shrieks Saffi.

I look up. Jack's dad is lying on the ground on the other side of the crack. I think he's been knocked unconscious by a falling branch.

Saffi tries to reach him, but she can't. The crack is growing too *quickly*.

And we might be in trouble. The diplodocus is turning. It's coming back towards us.

'We need to move,' says Jack.

'What about Dad?' says Saffi.

He's almost fifty metres away now, a gigantic yawning chasm opening up between us.

'We can't get to him,' says Jack. 'And if we don't move, we're going to get **squashed**!'

He's right. The diplodocus is heading straight for us. And it's breaking into a trot. We're in imminent danger of a squishing.

'Come on!' shouts Jack. He pulls Saffi to her feet, and we start *sprinting* towards the beach.

'Boys,' moans Saffi. 'Why do they *always* have to cause problems?'

CHAPTER SEVEN
Backwards Thinking

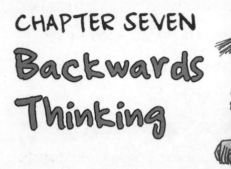

'I think it's gone,' Jack whispers.

We're hiding in a **narrow** cave at the end of the beach, huddled together in the dark. The microraptor is huddled right next to us. I think it's adopted us as pets.

We hold our breath and listen. The diplodocus is still thundering through

the forest. But its footsteps are getting quieter. We're safe, for now. Who knows what we're going to bump into next?

'Idiots,' growls Saffi.

'Pardon?' says Jack.

'*Idiots!*' repeats Saffi. 'The pair of you!' She stands up and starts **angrily** dusting off her pyjamas.

'Why couldn't you have kept your mouths shut?' she **SNAPS**. 'Everyone knows about the Captain Saurus curse.'

'I thought you didn't believe in it,' says Jack.

'So?' says Saffi, swivelling around and glaring at him. 'What's that got to do with anything? Obviously it *is* true, and *you two* were the idiots who activated it.'

'Actually,' I say, rather quietly, 'that's not *entirely* accurate.'

Saffi eyeballs me. 'What are you trying to say?' she growls.

'Well,' I say, knees shaking a little, 'it was you who said his name the third time.'

Saffi narrows her eyes and stalks towards me. 'Are you saying this is all *my* fault?'

I gulp. Teenagers are a lot **scarier** than dinosaurs. I'm in big trouble.

'Er . . .' I mutter.

She backs me up against the cave wall. Her face is right next to mine. 'And I suppose it's my fault you two found that $stupid$ eyeball as well?'

Suddenly a light bulb goes on in

my head. 'The eyeball,' I say. 'That's it!'

'What's it?' snaps Saffi, furling her brow.

'The writing on the eyeball,' I say. 'It's not Latin. *It's backwards!*'

I'm such a custard brain. Why didn't I think of it before?

Saffi turns to Jack. 'Your four-eyed friend has finally lost it,' she says.

But Jack ignores her. He's grinning

with excitement. He's

thinking the same thing as me. Jack pulls the box out of his pocket and takes

out the eyeball. We crowd around and peer through it.

'You're right, Toby,' says Jack.

And I am right. The writing isn't spelt wrong. It's just spelt backwards. You have to look *through* the eyeball to read it.

'TO REVERSE THE CURSE,' reads Jack, 'GIVE BACK WHAT IS MINE.'

'What's that supposed to mean?' asks Saffi.

'The eyeball!' I say. 'If we give it back to Captain Saurus, he'll reverse the curse. Everything will return to normal!'

'But how are we meant to give it back to him?' says Saffi. 'He's *dead*, in case you haven't noticed.'

I had noticed. He lived over a hundred years ago, so it would be rather **odd** if he wasn't.

'Hang on,' says Jack. 'There's something else.'

We gather around. There's a secret panel in the back of the box. It must have **cracked** open when Jack fell over. There's a piece of paper hidden inside. A secret pirate clue!

Jack unfolds the paper as quickly as he can. He has to be careful. The paper is old, brown and crumbly. It looks ancient.

'It's a map!' Jack gasps.

I can't believe it! A real pirate map! There's writing scrawled on the back:

The secret map of Captain Saurus. World Famous P.

It doesn't say anything after the

P because the map's RIPPED down the middle. The other half is missing, but that doesn't matter. This will be the half we need, I'm sure of it!

'What does it say?' I gabble. 'Where do we have to go?' I LOVE pirate maps.

'It doesn't,' says Jack. He looks confused.

'What do you mean it doesn't?' I ask.

Jack looks at me, utterly bamboozled. 'It's blank,' he says.

He passes me the map. Jack's right.

The front of the map is completely blank. No lines, no crosses: nothing. Just four more words scrawled in the top left corner. '**For my eyes only**,' it reads.

'Give me that!' Saffi snatches the paper out of my hand. 'Brilliant,' she snaps. 'Well, that's a fat lot of use. What are we supposed to do now?'

But no-one's got any answers. We just stand there, silent. Even the microraptor.

'There's only one thing we can do,' says Jack.

'What?' Saffi and I ask.

'We're going to have to think like a pirate.'

CHAPTER EIGHT
Seeing Things Differently

'AAARRRR,' I say.

'*AAAAaaarrrrr!*' says Jack.

We sound a bit like pirates. But it's not helping. The map's still blank, and we still don't know what to do.

We're sitting cross-legged on the floor. Saffi's pacing up and down

behind us. She doesn't want to think like a pirate. I did ask, but she was fairly clear about it.

'Maybe if you put Monty on your shoulder?' I suggest.

'Monty?' asks Jack.

'The microraptor.' I point at him. He's **hopping** around in the corner, munching beetles. I think Monty is a great name for him. He looks like a Monty.

'No,' says Jack, 'I don't think that will help. He doesn't have enough feathers, and he can't talk. Pirate-parrots are supposed to talk.'

He's right. Monty might be small, but he's definitely not a parrot. Although I might be able to teach him to talk. Microraptors were one of the cleverest

dinosaurs ever. In the Cretaceous period, they came **top** of the class.

'Right,' says Jack, 'we need to get serious.' He cups his chin in his hands. 'What do pirates want?'

'Treasure,' I say. 'Or booty. Either will do.'

'Okay,' says Jack. 'And they like keeping their booty to themselves, yes?'

'They certainly do,' I reply.

Pirates were dreadful at sharing. A bit like my baby brother, Louis. I'm not even allowed to *touch* his toys. Louis would make a **brilliant** pirate.

'So that's why the map says "*For my eyes only*",' says Jack. 'He doesn't want anyone else to look at it.'

Jack's got a point. But I don't think that helps. There's nothing on the map, so I'm not sure why anyone would want to look at it.

'For his eyes only . . .' mutters  Saffi. ' . . . for *his* eyes only! Duh,' she groans. 'We're being completely thick!' She tugs an elastic band out of her hair. 'Where is it?' she asks.

'What?' says Jack.

'The eyeball, bird brain. Hand it over!'

Jack holds up the eyeball. Saffi snatches it

out of his hand and starts twisting the hair band around it. Jack and I watch her, completely **puzzled**.

'There,' says Saffi, admiring her handiwork. She advances towards me. 'Now, put this on.' She **stretches** out the hair band.

'What are you doing?' I ask, taking a step backwards.

'Do you want to be a pirate or not?' she snaps.

'Er . . . yes,' I mumble.

'Then put it on!' She grabs my head, whips off my glasses and starts stretching the hair band over my scalp. It's a very **tight** fit. My brains are

about to get **SQUISHED** out of my nostrils.

'We need to position it right,' mutters Saffi. She starts tugging the hair band to the left, pulling my hair out in the process.

'Ow!' I yelp.

'Shhh!' she snips. 'Don't fuss.'

CLONK!

The eyeball plonks into my eye socket. It's uncomfortable. I've already got an eyeball in there. There isn't room for two.

'Now look at the map,' says Saffi.

'Pardon?'

She rolls her eyes. '*Look at the map!* It's for his eyes only. So use his eye to look at it!'

I scan the piece of paper. Suddenly it all makes sense.

'I can see something!' I say.

'What?' asks Jack.

'A map,' I say, tingling all over with excitement. ᴰ🄾ᵗˢ and ᴸⁱⁿᵉˢ and markings. And a cross! A great big cross!'

I can't believe it. Saffi was right. We needed to look at the map through Captain Saurus's eyes. That's why he hid the map with the eyeball!

'But how does it work?' asks Jack.

And that's when it hits me.

'Ultraviolet!' I say. 'Ultraviolet light. This map is written with invisible ink!'

It's probably lemon juice. In the old days pirates and spies used lemon juice to write secret messages. You could only read what it said if you heated the paper, or used ultraviolet light. And that's how Captain Saurus could see his enemies at night. Ultraviolet light picks up movement, even in the dark! That's how hawks and eagles can hunt from high up in the air. They can see in ultraviolet too!

I look over at Monty. He winks at me. He knew the answer all along. 'Right,' I say, 'let's go.' 'Where?' says Jack. I put my finger on the map. 'The **big** hill behind Camp Saurus. That's where the cross on the map says we should go.'

X marks the spot! Now we really are proper pirates.

CHAPTER NINE
Back to Camp Saurus

All four of us peek out of the cave.

'There's nothing there,' says Jack.

I'll have to take his word for it.
I can't see things in the distance. That's
why I wear glasses.

'Here,' says Saffi. 'Put these back
on.'

She hands me back my glasses.
Saffi's tied another hair band to the

handles. She stretches them over my head. The eyeball **clonks** against the right lens.

'Wouldn't it be simpler if Jack wears the eyeball?' I say.

'No,' says Saffi. 'If I have to trust my life to an eight-year-old, I'd rather it was one with a brain.'

Jack gives her a look. He's not too happy. But there's no point arguing. Teenagers are impossible, that's what Grandma says. And anyway, there's no denying she's got a point. I do have quite a big brain. I can't help it.

I inherited it from my mum.

I look out across the beach. It's amazing. I can see all kinds of things I'd never see without the eyeball. Birds flitting in the trees. Crabs **crawling** over the sand. I'm like Superman.

'Let's go,' I say.

We start jogging across the sand, Monty scampering along behind us. We need to go all the way back up through the woods and past the camp site. That's

73

where the 'X' on the map is.

'We should have a code word,' says Jack, 'in case we see another dinosaur.'

'Good idea,' I say. 'How about "dinosaur"?'

'No,' says Jack. 'Too many syllables. By the time we say it, we'll probably be eaten already.'

'Right,' I say. I have a think. 'Then how about "ＳＡＵＳＡＧＥ"?'

Jack considers this for a moment. 'Sausage it is,' he confirms.

'Idiots,' mutters Saffi.

We reach the end of the beach and start *climbing up* through the woods. This is where we saw the diplodocus. There could be other dinosaurs around, so we need to be super careful.

'Let's tiptoe,'
I whisper.

Everyone follows my
command. Even Saffi. She
might think we're idiots, but she
still doesn't want to get eaten.

I can see movement all around
me. Ants and bugs and
flies and frogs. This
eyeball is amazing. No
wonder Captain Saurus
could see so well. But
it's making me a little
bit jumpy. Every
time a butterfly goes past
I think it's a dinosaur,
and my stomach does a
somersault.

'I hope Dad's okay,' says Saffi.

So do I. I hope he hasn't been eaten. I won't have a clue what to say.

We reach the top of the hill and start tiptoeing towards the camp site. There's no sign of the diplodocus. But I'm keeping an eyeball out for it.

'Look,' says Jack. 'Up there.' He points off into the distance.

The crack in the earth has got bigger. It's **ENORMOUS** now. About thirty metres across. Right in the middle of it is a tall thin pinnacle of rock. It must have **spl it** off from the other side of the chasm. There's something lying on top of it. Something almost two metres long wearing bright yellow swimming trunks.

'That's Dad, isn't it?' says Saffi.

I nod. There's no mistaking those swimming trunks. You could see those things a mile away, even without a magic eyeball.

'Is he still alive?' asks Saffi.

I peer through the eyeball. I can see his **belly moving**. Either he's swallowed a wombat or he's breathing. I'm betting on the second one.

'We've got to get him down,' says Saffi.

But that's not going to be as simple as it sounds. Because suddenly we're surrounded. There's movement everywhere. And this time, it's definitely not butterflies.

'What is it?' asks Jack.

',' I hiss.

Jack and Saffi freeze. Monty cringes.

'What sort of sausage?' whispers Jack.

I peer into the bushes. It's difficult to see. There are so many of them. They're all **blurring** together.

'Is it another diplodocus?' asks Jack. 'A stegosaurus?'

I shake my head. It's something smaller. And a whole lot scarier. I look again, just to make sure. I can see skinny tails, sharp teeth and beady black eyes. And claws. Long, curved claws. One on each foot.

'It's deinonychuses,' I say.

CHAPTER TEN
Hitching a Ride

'Quick,' says Jack, 'climb up a tree.'

Monty doesn't need asking twice. He pegs it up a eucalypt as *fast* as his little legs will carry him.

'Why do we need to climb a tree?' asks Saffi.

'Because the deinonychuses are coming,' says Jack.

'So what?' says Saffi. 'What are they going to do?'

'Tear open your tummy and eat up your innards,' says Jack.

Saffi stares at him for a moment. 'Let's climb a tree,' she says.

We sprint over to Monty's tree and start pulling ourselves onto the branches. And not a moment too soon.

The deinonychuses burst out of the bushes, snarling and screeching and *snapping* their teeth. They leap up towards us, scraping great tears out of the bark with their terrible claws.

'Why are these things here?' squeals Saffi, as a **LETHAL** claw narrowly misses her ankle.

'Captain Saurus,' says Jack. 'He must have collected their bones.'

'Why didn't he collect gold and silver like any normal pirate?' shrieks Saffi.

Jack shrugs.

'Good taste, I guess.'

We clamber up on to the top branches of the tree. Monty's already sitting there. He looks remarkably calm. I suppose he's used to things trying to kill him.

The deinonychuses keep leaping up towards us. It's like being circled by wolves, but they're a lot less **cuddly**.

'Hey, five eyes,' says Saffi. 'What's that thing over there?'

I think she's talking to me. I look to where she's pointing. There's a great big beast lumbering towards us.

'It's an ankylosaurus,' says Jack.

He can see it too. And that's because it's pretty difficult to miss. It's like a **PREHISTORIC**

83

tank, covered from head to foot in armour, and with a huge bony club at the end of its tail. The deinonychuses are giving it a wide berth. It might be tasty, but it packs a punch.

'Gosh,' I say, 'it really is fossil central around here.'

All of a sudden we hear a screeching noise from out over the canyon. It's the deinonychuses. They've sniffed out Jack's dad. They're throwing themselves at the pinnacle of rock and trying to

scrape up to the top with their claws.

We're running out of time.

'Right,' says Saffi, 'that does it.' She starts pulling up her sleeves. 'Now you're certain if we return the eyeball, the **curse** will be lifted, yes?'

'Yes,' Jack and I say.

'And then everything will go back the way it was?' asks Saffi.

'Yes.'

'Fine.' She moves towards the edge of the branch. 'Then hold onto my legs.'

'What –' begins Jack.

'Just hold onto my legs!' Saffi hooks her feet around a knot of wood and dives off the branch, right into the range of the **biting** deinonychuses!

'What are you doing?' shouts Jack. 'They're going to get you!'

'Then stop whining and hold onto me!' barks Saffi.

We do what we're told. All three of us. I've no idea what Saffi's doing. Maybe she's gone mad? She's scrabbling with her hands, trying to grab hold of something below us.

I peer down with the eyeball. And I see it. One of the ropes from the teepee! It must have been thrown into the tree

by the racing diplodocus. I think Saffi's onto something!

RRRRRRR . . .

One of the deinonychuses has spotted Saffi. It grins, showing its vicious little teeth. It scratches its claws in the dirt, like a bull about to charge. And then it races towards us.

'Quickly!' shouts Jack.

Saffi stretches downwards. 'I've got it!' she cries. 'Pull me up!'

We start pulling on her legs, but she's awfully **heavy**.

'Get on with it!' barks Saffi.

The deinonychus is closing in. Its horrible black claws are hooked and ready.

NNNGGGG.

Jack and I strain with all our strength. And bit by bit we start reeling Saffi in.

'RRRRAAARRR!'

squeals the deinonychus. It digs one claw into the tree trunk and lunges upwards with the other.

OOF!

We heave Saffi back up over the branch. The deinonychus scrapes the air and **tumbles** down to the ground.

'Take your time, why don't you,' snaps Saffi. She pulls up the rope and starts tying it up in a loop.

'What are you doing?' asks Jack.

'Saving the day, what else?' She finishes the knot and starts swinging the rope above her head. It's a lasso!

SHWING!

She releases the lasso. It flies out of the tree, straight as an arrow, and loops around the ankylosaurus's neck. Saffi's hitching us a ride!

'Yup', says Saffi, 'I've always said it.' She dusts herself off. 'Ten years of Pony Club has got to be good for something.'

CHAPTER ELEVEN
Giddy-Up-a-Saurus

Saffi ties the other end of the  rope

to the branch. 'That's a slip knot,' she says, pointing at it. 'When I pull hard at the other end, it'll come loose.' She reaches into her hair, pulls out three more hair bands, and hands one each to Jack and me.

'Gosh,' I say. 'You certainly have a lot of hair bands in there.'

Saffi winks at me. 'You can never have enough hair bands,' she says. 'First rule of Girl Scouts.'

I'll remember that. I'm a scout too. Although I'm not a girl.

'Now,' says Saffi, 'take your hair band,  it over the rope, and slide.'

I think she wants us to use the rope as a zipline.

'Um . . .' I say. Physical exercise isn't exactly my strong point.

Saffi shrugs. 'Your choice. It's either slide or get .'

She points down the tree. The

deinonychuses are still there. And we can't stay up here forever.

Oh, well. I suppose I've lived a good life for an eight-year-old. I loop my hair band over the rope and grip hold of both ends. Monty hops onto my shoulder.

Wow, I really am a pirate. Complete with glass eye and parrot. If only I were as brave as a pirate. That would really help right now. I take a deep breath. okay, I'll do it on three. One . . . two . . .

Saffi's right foot connects firmly with my bottom. Monty and I start sliding down the rope. Very, very fast.

I land nose first on the back of a very surprised ankylosaurus.

WHOMP!

Jack lands on top of me.

The ankylosaurus is not amused. It starts bucking and shaking. It's like rodeo-riding, Cretaceous-style. The deinonychuses stand back, watching us with hungry little eyes. One slip and we'll be dino snacks.

SHOOF.

Saffi lands on two feet behind us, perfectly balanced. She tugs loose the slip knot and yanks back on the ankylosaurus's neck.

'YAAA!' she hollers.

The ankylosaurus immediately stands still. It might be big, but it knows when to mind its manners. This girl is not to be messed with.

Saffi vaults into a sitting position, feet dangling over the ankylosaurus's shoulders. Jack and I sit s^ha^ki^ly behind her, Monty nestled in the middle.

'All right, Einstein,' says Saffi, 'which way are we going?'

Oh, yes. The map. I pull it carefully out of my pocket and inspect it through the eyeball.

'Straight on,' I say, 'back up the hill. We should come to a fence. Once we get over that, we'll be close to the "X".'

'Right,' says Saffi. She flicks the reins and the ankylosaurus trundles forward.

Jack turns around. 'Hang in there, Dad!' he shouts. 'We'll come back for you!'

CHAPTER TWELVE
X Marks the Spot

Archie the ankylosaurus grumpfles his way through the forest. Saffi's forced him into a trot, and I think he's feeling a bit **puffed**. He actually makes for quite a comfy ride. His armour is a bit hard on the buttocks, but he's very roomy. You could fit a whole class

of kids on his back. He'd make a great school bus!

'Here's the fence,' says Jack.

It looks more like a bundle of broken **STICKS**. The fence was built to keep animals out of the camp site, but it definitely wasn't diplodocus-proof.

I study the map. 'That way,' I say, pointing. 'To the top of the hill.'

We tromp along. The trees start getting thicker and thicker. I don't think many people wander this far into the **FOREST**. But I can

hear noises. Squawks and growls and grunts. Monty and Archie aren't the only dinosaurs around here.

'Now what?' says Jack.

We've come to a place where the trees are so huge we can't see past them. All we can see is a **tangled** curtain of twigs and leaves and branches.

'Straight through,' I say. 'The "X" is on the other side.'

Saffi kicks her heels and our ride rumbles forward. He's not happy. It's a tight squeeze for an ankylosaurus. The trees are poking him in all the places he doesn't have armour. It must be awfully tickly. But he doesn't even crack a smile.

GRRRRUFF.

Archie squeezes through. We've reached the other side. There's open air in front of us. Hooray! We're finally out of the woods.

'Oh dear,' says Jack.

I look down. There's open air beneath us as well. Not so hooray. It's

102

another crack in the earth, about nine metres deep. And we're dangling right above it.

'AIIIEEEEE!' we shriek, dropping down into the darkness. Steep cliffs of mud fly by on either side.

THUD!

We land with a teeth-shuddering thump. Archie grunts and gives himself a shake. He doesn't seem too fussed about the fall. He must have very strong legs.

'Where on earth are we?' says Saffi.

We're not on earth. We're *under* the earth, in a crack made by the **stomping** diplodocus. I survey the map. This is exactly where we're supposed to be. 'X' marks the spot.

'What's that?' Jack asks, pointing ahead.

It's hard to see. We're on a crumbly underground platform, enclosed within steep rocky walls. The walls almost meet high above us, blocking out the light. But there's definitely something there. It's a tiny wooden hut, ancient, black and twisted. It must be over a hundred years old.

This must be the place.

'Okay,' says Saffi. 'Let's go.'

She urges Archie forward. He moves slowly. You can tell he's a bit **nervous**.

'Eek!' chirrups Monty. He's nervous too.

It's dark and musty and dusty down here. It's super scary. But at least there aren't any huge ugly meat-eating monsters.

ROOOOAAAR!

. . . I spoke too soon.

CHAPTER THIRTEEN
One-Eyed Rex

The monster emerges out of the shadows.

It's huge. Its head is so large it could swallow a car without chewing. It stops in front of us, its **massive** clawed feet digging into the earth. Then it raises its head and roars a roar that shakes the entire canyon.

'Do you know what?' sighs Saffi. 'I've had just about enough of dinosaurs.'

The monster lowers its head and growls. It's got one eye, which *glitters* bright green like an emerald. The other eye is missing, the socket covered with a flap of skin.

'I can't believe it,' says Jack.

'What?' I say.

'It's One-Eyed Rex,' says Jack.

'One-Eyed who?' I ask.

'One-Eyed Rex. Legend has it he was the most frightening of all Captain Saurus's crew.'

I'm not so sure about that. One-Eyed Rex doesn't look like a scary pirate. He looks like a scary tyrannosaurus.

A big,  one that's about to eat us. Which is a shame. The last tyrannosaurus I met was much friendlier.

'What do we do?' asks Jack.

We need to get into the hut. But that also means getting past One-Eyed Rex. And he doesn't look open to negotiation.

'Right,'  Saffi. 'It's time to put an end to this.' She gets a good grip on Archie's reins and leans forward. 'You need to get into that hut, yes?'

'Er . . . yes,' I reply.

'Fine. Then get ready to jump.'

I'm about to ask what she means, but I don't have time. Saffi boots Archie into a gallop and bellows a battle charge.

'YAAAAA!'

We thunder straight towards One-Eyed Rex. Archie roars, Monty shrieks, and Jack and I scream. It's the *craziest* plan in the universe.

But it works!

One-Eyed Rex wasn't expecting an attack. His jaws crunch closed but he's too slow. We gallop between his legs, barging the beast to one side.

Archie *skids* to a stop, scattering dust in all directions.

'Jump!' shouts Saffi. 'Go!'

I look around. We're right next to the hut. We can make it!

'But what are you going to do?' asks Jack.

'I'm going to deal with ol' Blinky over there.' She nods at One-Eyed Rex.

The tyrannosaurus has turned around and he looks **furious**. But Saffi doesn't flinch. She eyeballs

him, jaws clenched. Saffi's not scared of pirates. Even prehistoric ones.

'Now go,' growls Saffi.

One-Eyed Rex takes a step forward.

'But –' starts Jack.

'*GO!*' roars Saffi.

One-Eyed Rex starts to charge. Saffi bellows in reply and urges Archie forward. Jack and I tumble off Archie's back and race towards the hut, Monty scampering behind us.

The mighty dinosaurs meet with a bone-splitting crunch.

I spin around, one hand on the door. Rex scrapes at Saffi with his claws. Archie thumps him aside with his club.

It's a battle of giants!

Saffi turns to look at us, face flushed. 'Get in there!' she shouts, 'and give Captain Saurus back that eyeball!'

We open the door and *race* into the hut.

CHAPTER FOURTEEN
Riddles and Bones

'There's nothing in here,' says Jack.

He's right. Apart from a few bones scattered across the floor, the hut's empty.

'Whose bones are those?' asks Jack.

'They probably belong to children,' I say. 'The last ones in here before us.'

Jack gulps. 'We better work *fast*,' he says.

We start investigating. It's dark and **smelly**. What are we supposed to do? Where's the 'X'?

'Hang on,' says Jack. 'What's that?' He points over at the corner.

There's a rough wooden disc sticking out of the floor. It's got three shapes carved into it: a circle, a square and a **triangle**. They look like giant keyholes. But where are the keys?

'Wait, I think I can see something.'
My eyes are adjusting to the darkness.
'Writing,' I say. 'There's writing on the walls!'

'What does it say?' asks Jack.

He can't see it. It's written in **invisible** ink, just like the markings on the map.

I close my left eye and peer through the eyeball. There are three lines of writing, each with a shape drawn next to it. They look like riddles.

'They must be clues,' I say. 'The shapes on the wall match the ones on the disc.'

'And the bones are the keys!' says Jack, picking one of them up. 'These aren't children's bones, they're dinosaur bones.'

He's right. The bone he's holding

is .

No children have bones that big. Apart from Doris Codswallop. But I'm pretty sure she's still alive. I saw her on the swings on Friday.

CRASH!

All of a sudden something smashes through the wall. It's Rex's head.

'Take that, you one-eyed freak!' squeals Saffi.

I think she just scored a hit. The hut rattles and shakes as a roaring Rex pulls his head back out. We need to hurry. I don't think this hut will stay standing for long.

'Quickly,' says Jack, 'read the first riddle!'

I squint through the eyeball. The writing's super **messy**, but I can just about make out what it says:

I am a Tyrant first, a Lizard Second, and a King Third.

Jack grins. 'That's easy,' he says. 'It's a tyrannosaurus rex!'

Of course! Tyranno-Saurus-Rex = Tyrant-Lizard-King. That's what the name means in Latin.

'This must be the key!' Jack holds up a huge *jagged* tooth.

'It's a tyrannosaurus tooth, I'm sure of it!' He races over to the disc. I hope it isn't Rex's tooth. He might want it back. 'Which shape is it?' shouts Jack.

I look up at the wall. 'It's the first one, the circle!'

Jack pushes the tooth into the keyhole.

The disc rotates to the left. A crack starts opening in the floor. There's something down there!

'Okay, what's next?' asks Jack.

Archie's tail explodes through the wall, stopping millimetres from my nose.

'Get a move on!' screams Saffi. 'I can't hold him off for long!'

'Read the second clue!' shouts Jack.

I peer at the wall and read out:

Jack stares at me. 'What's that supposed to mean?'

Archie thunders into the side of the hut. A plank comes loose from the ceiling and bonks me on the head.

'A velociraptor!' I say. 'That's what its name means. Speedy Thief!'

'Brilliant!' says Jack. He starts rifling through the bones. 'This one!' he shouts. 'It's a velociraptor claw!'

CRASH!

The roof explodes inwards. Jack and I collapse to the floor. Monty leaps aside with a squawk. Rex's jaws crunch closed right where our heads just were. I think he's discovered our hiding place.

'Get away from my brother, you overgrown gecko!' *screams* Saffi.

Archie rams into Rex's side. Time is definitely running out.

Jack pushes the velociraptor claw into the keyhole. The disc rotates a

little more, but we still can't see what's down there.

'Okay,' says Jack, 'last one. What's the riddle?'

I start reading:

There are three reasons not to attack me. Get the point?

Jack looks confused. 'Get what point?' he asks.

'*The* point,' I say. 'That's the riddle. That's what it says.'

'But that doesn't make any sense!' yells Jack.

KABOOM!

The whole hut disintegrates around us. Chunks of wood go flying past my head.

I look up. One-Eyed Rex is towering over us. Archie is lying on his side on the ground, breathing heavily. He's got a huge tear in his side.

'Hurry!' screams Saffi. *'Hurry!'* She's trapped under Archie's tail.

We're on our own.

Rex opens his mouth and roars. A huge **earth-shattering** roar of triumph. Then he leans down

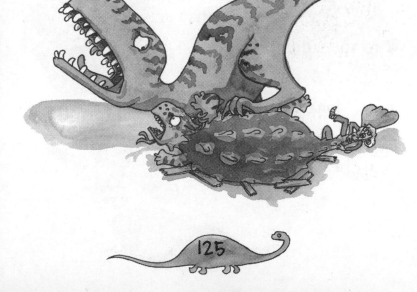

125

and looks at us. It's all over. We're finished.

SQUAWK!

Something's rubbing against my leg. It's Monty. Poor little beastie. He must be terrified too. He's holding something in his mouth. Some sort of horn.

'That's it!' shouts Jack, staring at Monty. 'Triceratops horns. They had three of them – and they all had points!'

We've got the answer to the riddle! Pointy horns! Monty did it!

Jack grabs the horn, bends down and pushes it into the disc.

rUMBLE.

The floor starts crumbling open.

ROAAAARRRR!

I look up. Rex is opening his mouth to strike. We've got seconds left!

'Quickly!' shouts Jack. 'The eyeball!'

I turn back and look at him. There's a skeleton under the floor. It's wearing an old red jacket and a jaunty black hat. And it's got a patch over one eye.

It's Captain Saurus!

'THROW IT!' yells Jack. 'NOW!'

Rex's head starts descending. He's metres away. I pull the eyeball over my head and throw it to Jack.

But I'm not going to make it. Rex's teeth are closing in around me. My final moments have come! I'll never be an astronaut now. THE END IS FINALLY HERE.

AAAAARGH!

CHAPTER FIFTEEN
Last Piece of the Puzzle

I open my eyes.

It's silent. Completely silent. Am I dead? Is this the afterlife? If so, where's my space rocket? I thought everyone got a space rocket in the afterlife?

'We did it!' says Jack. 'We lifted the curse!'

I look around me. We're back on solid ground. The **crack** in the earth has disappeared. And so have the dinosaurs. Jack returned the eyeball just in time!

I rush over to Captain Saurus's grave. He's staring up at me, his eyeball glittering in its bony socket. I bet he's glad to have it back. No-one likes it when their eyeball goes missing.

CREAK.

Captain Saurus's hand starts opening.

'Yikes!' yelps Jack.

We both leap backwards. Are his bones coming back to life? Are we about to be attacked by a skeleton? Wasn't a

one-eyed tyrannosaurus scary enough?

But nothing happens. We tiptoe back to the grave. He's holding something. It looks like a piece of paper. A piece of old, brown, crumbly paper. I think he wants us to take it.

Jack looks at me. 'Your turn,' he says. 'I did the eyeball.'

I take a deep breath. Then I lean down and pick up the paper.

CRUMBLE.

The whole grave starts collapsing inwards. I pull my hand out just in time. Captain Saurus has gone. He's disappeared back under the earth.

'What does it say?' asks Jack.

Oh, yes. The paper. I carefully open it. It's a map. A proper one. With lines and dots and markings.

'*Alaeontologist*,' says the writing at the top.

'Alaeontologist?' asks Jack. 'What's that supposed to mean?'

I pull out the other map from my pocket. The one that brought us here. I hold the two halves of the map together. It's a perfect match!

'The Secret Map of Captain Saurus,

132

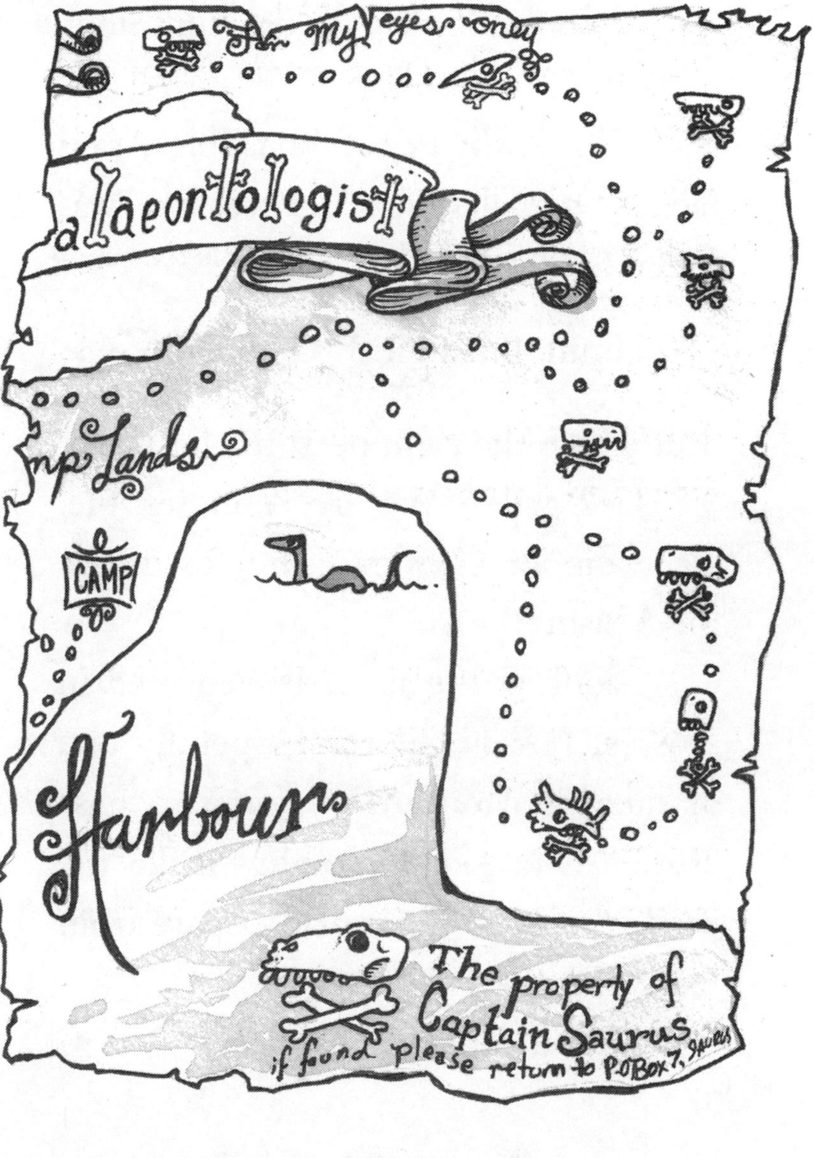

For my eyes only
alaeontologist
np Lands
CAMP
Harbour
The property of
Captain Saurus
if found please return to P.O Box 7, Saurus

World Famous Palaeontologist,' it reads.

Captain Saurus was a palaeontology pirate!

'That's why he set the riddles,' says Jack. 'To make sure his treasure was found by the right person!'

Hmm. I'm a bit *puzzled*.

'But who *is* the right person?' I ask.

Jack grins. 'We are. You and me. True dinosaur lovers. The fossils are the treasure!'

I look at the map. It's covered in crosses. Fossils galore! Hopefully one of them is Monty. I'm going to miss him. Archie too. Dinosaurs make the best friends in the world. Apart from Jack, of course.

'There you are!'

It's Jack's dad. He's
running towards us
and he's still wearing
his banana-yellow
swimming trunks.
'Has it gone?' he

'Has what gone?'
asks Jack.

'The Lesser-
Spotted Gibber Lizard.
I found my camera,
but then I must have nodded off!'

Jack winks at me. 'Yes, Dad,' he
says. 'It's gone. They've all gone.'

Jack's dad gasps. 'You mean there
was more than one? Which way did
they go?'

Jack points into the bushes and his dad scampers off, camera at the ready.

'Grown-ups.' Jack smiles. 'They're not very clever, are they?'

GRUEEEEER.

A rumbling groan comes from behind us. Oh no. It's One-Eyed Rex. We've been tricked!

But it's not One-Eyed Rex. It's a hideous, staggering zombie with *tangled* hair, torn clothes and

mud smeared across its face. It lurches towards us.

Jack and I take a step backwards. The zombie stops, laughs and puts its arms around our shoulders.

'And there I was thinking camping was going to be boring,' it says, 'but nothing's boring with you two along for the ride.'

It's not a zombie. It's Saffi. And she just did something amazing.

She just smiled.

Sometimes legends really do come true.

Saurus Street is just like any other street . . . except for the dinosaurs.

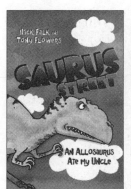

Collect them all!

Watch out for
Billy is a Dragon
by Nick Falk
and Tony Flowers
coming in March 2014